FEELING LEFT OUT

The First in a Series Children's Books from the Executive Director of HandiCapableFitness.com

James Norris

AuthorHouse™
1663 Liberty Drive
Bloomington, IN 47403
www.authorhouse.com
Phone: 833-262-8899

Because of the dynamic nature of the Internet, any web addresses or links contained in this book may have changed since publication and may no longer be valid. The views expressed in this work are solely those of the author and do not necessarily reflect the views of the publisher, and the publisher hereby disclaims any responsibility for them.

This book is printed on acid-free paper.

ISBN: 978-1-6655-6936-1 (sc)
ISBN: 978-1-6655-7869-1 (hc)
ISBN: 978-1-6655-7868-4 (e)

Library of Congress Control Number: 2022923545

Print information available on the last page.

Published by AuthorHouse   12/19/2022

authorHOUSE®

DEDICATION

I am dedicating *Feeling Left Out* to Judy Colella (Mrs. C). The late Mrs. C was my one-on-one paraprofessional from kindergarten through eighth grade. This is the time period where my first of four (4) books takes place.

Mrs. C was much more than a paraprofessional! She was the true definition of a teacher and a mentor.

Mrs. C had one of the biggest hearts but yet she also knew when to hold me accountable and not let me off the hook when I was trying to pull a fast one.

Many of the lessons she taught me I still use today as I aim to mentor the next generation. This Dedication of Book #1 of 4 is just a small token of my appreciation and a way of ensuring her legacy lives on for years to come. Thank you Mrs. C!

ACKNOWLEDGMENTS

Feeling Left Out was made possible thanks to the following:

My Lord and Savior, Jesus Christ, who deserves credit for everything I do.

My family, especially to my parents, Jay and Lisa, for giving me life and equipping me with the tools I need to succeed. You gave me more love than anyone could ever ask for.

My amazing team of educators—in particular, Ronna Thur, Debbie Bompane, Dick Crump, Steve Williams, Ed Carey, and Dominick Indindoli. Even when we disagreed, you believed in me and pushed me to make something of myself.

My best friend and mentor, Erica Walker, for leading by example and with compassion and friendship. You have left a giant footprint on my heart!

Handi Capable Fitness Board Members Kenny Whittier, James Ward, and Jason Rossi. Special thanks to Paul Solano and the Adelaide Breed Bayrd Foundation for making this project a reality.

My friends Craig Seidenglanz, Marco Corrado, Alex Guarco, and the Martignetti family.

And of course, all of the Handi Capable athletes, donors, and supporters! This dream came true because of you! Thank you!

--

James Norris
(Handi Capable Fitness)

Platinum Extraordinaire Sponsor: The Adelaide Breed Bayrd Foundation

Platinum Sponsor: Enjet Aero Corporation of Malden, Massachusetts

Gold Sponsor: The Lapenta family
              The Ward family

Silver Sponsor: Cliff Cunningham

Bronze Sponsor: Jackie Bouley
Doreen Burke
Doug Hawkins
Tom Pizzo
The Sholl family
The Solano family
Douglas Tran

It was a warm spring day at Barrows Elementary School in Reading, Massachusetts.

The birds were singing, and all Jimmy's classmates were screaming with excitement as they played tag on the playground.

Jimmy was off to the side with his favorite teacher, Mrs. C., feeling very sad and left out. He wished so much that he could play too.

Jimmy was unable to play because his legs were weak, and he had to use a wheelchair to move around.

Jimmy could not keep up with all the other kids. Jimmy would often ask, "Why do I have to use this dumb wheelchair?

It's so slow. I can't keep up with all the other kids. Oh, and I have to ride on a special bus too! Grrr. I just want to be one of the cool kids, even just for a day!"

Now, right as Jimmy was about to cry and fake being sick so he could go home and watch cartoons, Jimmy's classmate Steve ran by and saw a tear slowly running down Jimmy's cheek.

Oh no—I wonder what's wrong with Jimmy, thought Steve. Should I go up and talk to him? What if he gets even more upset and yells at me to leave him alone? No, I can't do it!

Then he told himself, *Yes, you can! Remember that time you were sad and Trandon asked you to play a game and you felt so much better after? Yeah? Well, go ahead—go talk to Jimmy!*

Steve was so scared as he walked up to Jimmy to see why he was so upset. His hands were shaking, and his belly was rumbling. "Hey, Jimmy," Steve whispered, "are you OK? I saw that you were crying. What's wrong?"

Steve waited very nervously as he waited for Jimmy to answer. Then Jimmy said, "I'm fine; you won't understand!"

"Wait, what won't I understand?" asked Steve.

Jimmy answered, "I just want to fit in! But instead, I have to use a wheelchair, and it's just not fair. I just want to be one of the cool kids and play tag with everyone!"

Steve said, "Well, I don't know what it's like to use a wheelchair, but I stutter when I get really nervous. So I kind of understand how you feel. But you are definitely a cool kid! Jimmy, you have your own car that you can drive in school, and you have a horn you can scare the teachers with!" Both boys laughed, and Steve blurted out, "I wish I had one!"

Jimmy smiled and said, "So you really think I'm a cool kid?"

"Yes, you are!" yelled Steve with a huge smile.

"Do you want to go play Go Fish before we have to get back to our schoolwork?"

"Let's go!" said Steve.

The best friends soon went inside and played three games, and Jimmy won all three! Steve also wanted to tell Jimmy a joke.

Knock, Knock.

Who's there?

Cows go.

Cows go who?

No, silly, cows go moo!

Jimmy laughed and exclaimed, "That's a good one!
Now it's my turn to tell one."

Knock, Knock

Who's there?

Mustache.

Mustache who?

Mustache you a question, but I'll shave it for later!

These two silly boys laughed until they cried. All their classmates came running over to see what was so funny. Jimmy told all the kids his joke, and they roared with laughter.

Mrs. C. said, "Kids say the darndest things! OK, everyone, back to class. It's time to do our math work."

The next day during free time, the entire class wanted Jimmy and Steve to tell more jokes.

They did, and everyone laughed again and again. And Steve and Jimmy are still best friends today!

Jimmy finally felt like a cool kid. He realized that the things that made him a little different from everyone else—like using a wheelchair to get around school—were actually pretty cool.

It was almost like he had superpowers.

Do you sometimes get sad like Jimmy because you want to be cool?

Well, Jimmy wants you to know that it doesn't matter whether you use a wheelchair like him or stutter like Steve; we all have superpowers that make us cool!

Never stop believing in yourself, and stop feeling left out.

THE END